The Deadly Nards

"Run!" Eva yelled.

It was too late. One of the aliens grabbed Ellen's arms.

Ellen kicked her feet with all her might. "Get off me! Let go!"

Lila tried to pry the alien's fingers off Ellen's arm. Jessica stomped on the alicn's foot. But it was no use.

"Where are you taking us?" Elizabeth demanded.

The aliens grunted something in what sounded like Zardian.

"They probably don't speak English," Andy said.

"Do you think they're taking us to the Nards?" Eva asked, struggling against the alien who was holding her.

Nobody answered that one.

Bantam Books in the SWEET VALLEY KIDS series

SWEET VALLEY KIDS
SUPER SNOOPER #7

THE CASE OF THE ALIEN PRINCESS

Written by
Molly Mia Stewart

Created by
FRANCINE PASCAL

Illustrated by
Ying-Hwa Hu

BANTAM BOOKS
NEW YORK • TORONTO • LONDON • SYDNEY • AUCKLAND

RL 2, 005-008

THE CASE OF THE ALIEN PRINCESS
A Bantam Book / June 1994

*Sweet Valley High® and Sweet Valley Kids are
trademarks of Francine Pascal*

Conceived by Francine Pascal

*Produced by Daniel Weiss Associates, Inc.
33 West 17th Street
New York, NY 10011*

Cover art by Susan Tang

ISBN: 0-553-48119-3

Published simultaneously in the United States and Canada

*Bantam Books are published by Bantam Books, a division of Bantam
Doubleday Dell Publishing Group, Inc. Its trademark, consisting of the
words "Bantam Books" and the portrayal of a rooster, is Registered in
U.S. Patent and Trademark Office and in other countries. Marca
Registrada. Bantam Books, 1540 Broadway, New York, New York 10036.*

PRINTED IN THE UNITED STATES OF AMERICA

CWO   0 9 8 7 6 5 4 3 2 1

To Sebastian Bobrick

CHAPTER 1

Close Encounter

B *rring! Brring!*
  "Someone get the phone!" Mrs. Wakefield yelled from the second floor.

Jessica looked out the Wakefields' kitchen window. Her father and older brother, Steven, were splashing in the family's aboveground swimming pool.

Jessica's twin sister, Elizabeth, was in the den. The twins were in the middle of watching a movie about a monster who eats Los Angeles. Jessica had run into the kitchen to get more popcorn. She didn't want to miss any of the movie, but it looked as if answering the phone was up to her.

Brring! Brring!

Jessica grabbed the phone. "Hello?" she said impatiently.

"This is Andy Franklin," the voice on the other end said. "May I speak to Elizabeth or Jessica, please?"

Andy was in the twins' class at school. His favorite subjects were math and science. He wore glasses that always fell off during gym class.

Elizabeth thought Andy was nice. Jessica had thought he was nerdy until Andy had proved his bravery on a class field trip. Ever since then Jessica liked Andy better. Still, she had never talked to him on the phone before. She wondered why he was calling now.

"Hi, Andy," Jessica said. "This is Jessica. What's up?"

"I made contact with an alien race!" Andy yelled.

"What?" Jessica said.

"Meet me at the park right away," Andy said.

"Is this some kind of joke?" Jessica asked. "Andy? Hello?"

Andy didn't answer. He had already hung up.

Jessica replaced the phone. "Mom," she yelled up the stairs. "Elizabeth and I are going to the park."

"OK, have fun," Mrs. Wakefield called back.

Jessica ran into the den. "Elizabeth, come on. We've got to get to the park. It's an emergency."

Elizabeth jumped up and turned off the television. While the twins pedaled their bikes toward Charles Fremont Park, Jessica told Elizabeth what Andy had said on the phone.

"That's mysterious," Elizabeth said when Jessica had finished.

Jessica nodded and grinned. She loved secrets and mysteries. Jessica and Elizabeth and some of their friends had even started a detective club called the Snoopers. They had solved lots of important cases.

The biggest mystery of all, though, was how Jessica and Elizabeth could be identical twins and still be so different from one another.

The two girls looked exactly alike. They both had blue-green eyes and long blond hair with bangs. When they wore identical outfits, the only way to tell them apart was by looking at their name bracelets.

Even though the twins looked the same on the outside, their personalities were very different. Elizabeth loved school and playing all kinds of sports. Jessica loved dolls and hated getting her clothes messy. Even though they were different in many ways, Jessica and Elizabeth were best friends.

They were also both great detectives.

"I was just thinking about Field Day," Elizabeth said.

"Me, too," Jessica said.

Field Day was a special event for the kids at Sweet Valley Elementary School. The whole school went to Secca Lake for a day of picnics and games. On the last Field Day, Elizabeth, Jessica, and some of the kids from their class had thought they had seen an alien in the woods. Only Andy wasn't fooled.

"Andy knows lots about UFOs," Elizabeth said.

"And creatures from outer space," Jessica added.

"Andy wouldn't say he met an alien, unless—" Elizabeth said.

"Unless he really *did* meet one," Jessica finished for her.

Elizabeth and Jessica turned their bikes into the park. A bunch of bikes were already pulled up under a big tree near the gate.

"That's Lila's," Jessica said, pointing to a bike with a banana seat and rainbow streamers coming out of the handlebars. Lila Fowler was Jessica's best friend after Elizabeth. She was also a Snooper.

"Everyone's here." Elizabeth started to run toward the swings. "Come on!"

Jessica could see Lila, Ellen Riteman, Amy Sutton, Eva Simpson, Todd Wilkins, and Winston Egbert—all of the rest of the Snoopers—sitting on or standing near the swings. They looked as if they were waiting for someone.

"What are you guys doing here?" Jessica asked.

"Andy called us and said to meet him at the park," Eva said.

"Something about aliens," Ellen said with a shudder.

"Aliens in Sweet Valley," Todd said. "Pretty cool, huh?"

"Out of this world!" Winston said.

6

Elizabeth giggled. "Do you guys seriously believe aliens would visit earth?"

"Sure," Amy said. "They might need a human for their zoo."

"Or slaves to polish their space suits," Lila suggested.

"Here comes Andy," Jessica said.

Andy was hurrying across the grass toward them. He kept pushing up his glasses as he ran.

"What's up?" Todd demanded as Andy came closer.

"About the alien, you mean?" Andy asked.

"Of course!" Jessica exclaimed.

"Well, it's pretty simple," Andy said. "My family went on a picnic at Secca Lake yesterday. I saw a spaceship and an alien."

"Wow," Winston breathed.

"What did the alien look like?" Elizabeth asked.

"It was about my size," Andy said. "And, um, green."

8

"Did you talk to it?" Ellen asked.

"Did you touch it?" Winston asked.

"Did *it* touch *you*?" Lila asked, inching farther away from Andy.

"No to all three questions," Andy said. "This is what happened: My family and I were eating lunch. I saw a creature hiding in a bush. It looked like it was listening to us. For a moment I studied the creature and it studied me. I noted its green skin and orange hair and realized it was from outer space.

"Then the alien started to run. I dropped my sandwich and ran after it. The alien had a good head start, and I started to lose it. But I kept running, hoping to catch up. After a minute or two I came to a clearing. That's when I saw the spaceship. It was just taking off."

The Snoopers' eyes were wide.

"I'm going back to the clearing tomorrow to see if the ship returns," Andy said.

9

"I want you guys to come to the lake with me and be witnesses in case anything happens."

"In case anything happens?" Jessica repeated.

"I don't think there's any danger," Andy said. "But I don't want to go alone."

"What do you think the alien wants?" Winston asked.

"To make friends," Andy said. "Or maybe it wants to learn more about our planet. What do you guys say? Will you come?"

The Snoopers exchanged looks.

"Elizabeth and I will be there," Jessica spoke up.

"Me, too," Eva said.

One by one Todd, Winston, Lila, and Amy promised to come.

Ellen sighed. "If everyone else is going, I guess I'll go, too." She did not look thrilled. Ellen was a bit of a chicken.

"Great," Andy said with a smile. "See you tomorrow."

Everyone headed home to get permission to go to the lake.

Mrs. Wakefield shook her head when the twins explained why the trip was so important. "A picnic at Secca Lake sounds fun," she said. "I'd be happy to go with you and your friends. But I do *not* believe in aliens."

Jessica felt goose bumps rise on her arms. What if her mother was wrong? What if aliens really *did* exist?

CHAPTER 2

Strange Visitors

"Do you see anything?" Elizabeth asked.

Amy shook her head without taking her eyes off the afternoon sky. "Nothing yet."

Andy and the Snoopers had been waiting in the clearing at Secca Lake for almost an hour. They hadn't seen any sign of an alien or a spaceship.

Elizabeth felt disappointed. Meeting creatures from another planet would be so awesome.

Amy, Todd, and Winston looked sad, too.

The rest of the Snoopers seemed relieved.

"I think your imagination ran away with you," Ellen told Andy.

"To Mars!" Lila said.

Jessica nodded. "Visitors from outer space. What a goofy idea."

"It is not goofy," Andy said. "I know they're going to come."

"How do you know?" Lila asked.

"It's a feeling I have," Andy told her. "I just know. If we wait, they'll come."

Ellen shrugged. "OK, we'll wait."

"But not too long," Lila said. "I hate to wait. It's boring."

"It won't be too long," Andy said.

But Andy and the Snoopers waited and waited. No spaceship came.

Lila, Jessica, and Ellen sat down in the middle of the clearing. Winston read a comic book. Andy kept scanning the sky. Eva, Amy, Todd, and Elizabeth poked around for clues.

"Hey, you guys," Elizabeth yelled. "We found something!"

Everyone ran over to Elizabeth. She showed them a little pile of sand.

"Big deal," Lila said. "It's just sand."

"Not just sand," Todd corrected Lila. "*Blue* sand."

Lila shrugged. "I think they have blue sand in Greece."

"But we're not in Greece," Amy pointed out.

"It could have come from someone's fish tank," Winston said.

Elizabeth sighed. "That's true."

"I think it's time for us to give up," Jessica told Andy. Elizabeth wanted to say she agreed, but she couldn't. She was too busy yawning to talk.

"I want to go back, too," Ellen said. "I'm so sleepy."

"You think *you're* sleepy," Andy said, sitting down in the grass. "I was up half the

14

night reading about space travel. I need a nap." Andy lay down and closed his eyes.

"You can't take a nap here," Todd said.

"Why not?" Ellen asked. She lay down, too.

"Get up!" Todd insisted. "You guys are too old for naps."

Andy and Ellen didn't seem to hear.

"They're asleep!" Amy exclaimed.

Jessica lay down, too. "Since we have to wait for Andy and Ellen, I think I'll catch forty—" Before Jessica could get out "winks," she was fast asleep.

One by one Lila, Eva, Winston, and Amy lay down and fell asleep.

"I can't—believe—everyone is—going to—sleep," Todd told Elizabeth. His words were interrupted by immense yawns. He fell asleep right where he was standing.

Elizabeth helped Todd lie down. Then she curled up in the grass and fell fast asleep, too.

Elizabeth sat up and glanced around the clearing. She didn't see anything unusual. But Elizabeth knew something had woken her up. She glanced *above* the clearing. What she saw there made her catch her breath.

Elizabeth shook Jessica. "Wake up!" she said.

Jessica sat up and rubbed her eyes. "What is it?"

Elizabeth pointed above her head.

"Wow," Jessica said, covering her mouth with her hand.

"Get everyone up," Elizabeth said. "Hurry!"

The twins woke up Andy and the rest of the Snoopers as fast as they could.

"That's it!" Andy shouted when he saw the object in the sky. "That's the ship!"

The Snoopers stared up in amazement as they got to their feet. A huge ship was

hovering over the clearing. It was the shape of a long, skinny triangle and it was the deepest black imaginable. The bright sunlight did not reflect off it. It made no noise.

"I think we better get out of here," Lila whispered.

"Let's go," Jessica agreed.

Before any of the Snoopers could take a step, a bright light shone on Elizabeth. She looked surprised for a second. Then she disappeared.

CHAPTER 3

All Aboard!

Jessica stared at the spot where Elizabeth had been standing a second before.

The others exchanged surprised looks.

"She's gone," Amy breathed.

"I don't think so." Todd pointed to the ship. "I think she's up there."

Winston's eyes were wide. "Come on! Let's get out of here."

"Good idea," Lila said, grabbing Jessica's hand and pulling her toward the trail.

"No!" Jessica yanked her hand back.

"I'm not leaving Elizabeth up there alone."

At that moment Jessica noticed all of her friends were staring at her. They looked terrified. Jessica got a funny feeling in her stomach. Her eyes were blinded by a bright light. Andy, Lila, and the others disappeared. The next thing Jessica saw was Elizabeth.

"Lizzie!" Jessica shouted.

"Jessica!" Elizabeth gave her sister a hug. "I'm so happy to see you."

"I'm happy to see you, too," Jessica said. "We thought you got zapped onto the spaceship."

"Look around!" Elizabeth exclaimed. "I think we're both on the ship."

"Really?" Jessica said, looking everywhere. "But this sure is a strange-looking spaceship."

The room the twins were standing in was empty except for rows of blinking lights. The floor, walls, and ceiling were all made from a dull silver metal. There were no tables or chairs. One wall had a huge window in it, but all the twins could see out of it was sky.

"It *is*—" Elizabeth started. But before she could get out "strange," Andy appeared.

"Andy!" Jessica exclaimed.

"You call this a spaceship?" Andy said with a frown. "What a gyp! Where are the computers and the control panels?"

Elizabeth managed a little laugh. "It doesn't look much like *Star Trek*."

Before Andy could complain any more, Amy appeared. After her the other Snoopers were zapped aboard one after another.

"Have you seen them?" Ellen whispered. She sounded afraid.

"Who?" Andy asked.

"The aliens," Ellen whispered, glancing over her shoulder.

"No," Andy said.

21

Ellen shuddered. "I hope they're not as ugly as E.T."

"E.T. isn't ugly," Eva said.

"He's hideous," Ellen insisted.

"What happens now?" Lila asked. "I'm getting bored."

Lila didn't stay bored for long. At that very second a door slid open and two aliens came in.

Lila jumped back and grabbed Ellen's arm.

The aliens weren't ugly. In fact, they had a strange beauty. They were about the same height as the Snoopers. Their skin was a faint green and looked soft and smooth. The aliens' eyes were a deep, deep green like cats'. One of the aliens had purple hair. The other one's hair was orange.

Jessica tried to keep an eye on both aliens. The one with orange hair went to stand against the wall. The other one

moved toward Andy and the Snoopers. They inched away. Even Andy seemed afraid.

Jessica sensed the ship had started to move at an incredible speed. The aliens were kidnapping them!

CHAPTER 4

A Strange New Friend

"Hello," the purple-haired alien said. The twins exchanged shocked glances.

"Hello," Elizabeth said.

The alien's face changed. It looked as if it was smiling!

Elizabeth forced herself to smile back.

"My name is Gazeal," the alien said.

"I'm Jessica," Jessica said.

"I'm Elizabeth," Elizabeth said.

The rest of the Snoopers rushed to introduce themselves.

Andy stepped forward last. "I am Andy

Franklin, citizen of the earth," he said. "At your service, sir—or, um, madam."

"Madam," Gazeal said with her strange smile. "On my planet all females have purple hair. Males have orange hair. That is how you can tell us apart."

The orange-haired alien stood near the wall, watching and listening.

"I can't believe you speak earthling!" Lila exclaimed.

Andy rolled his eyes. "For your information, Lila, there are hundreds of languages spoken on earth."

Gazeal smiled again. "Actually, the best estimates are approximately three thousand languages. That doesn't include dialects."

"How would you know?" Ellen demanded.

"I know a lot about the earth," Gazeal replied. "I checked a book about earth out of the library. We also visited your planet one earth-day ago. That's when I learned to speak English."

"You learned to speak English in a day?" Todd asked.

"Of course," Gazeal said. "I also mastered French, Arabic, and Chinese. You seem surprised. But of course you're surprised! I forgot about the size of your brains. On average, creatures on my planet are eight times as intelligent as earthlings."

"Eight times as intelligent?" Eva asked Gazeal.

"On average," the alien said. "But never mind. Your smaller brains have their advantages. For example, it makes you terrific at solving mysteries."

As soon as Gazeal mentioned mysteries, the orange-haired alien moved closer.

"This is all very interesting," Todd said. "But I'd like to know where you are taking us."

"Of course," Gazeal said calmly. "I am taking you to Venn. That is the name of my planet. My people—we are called

27

Zards—need your help solving an important mystery. I promise to return you to earth as soon as the mystery is solved."

The orange-haired alien stepped forward. "But if you fail to solve the mystery, you will never see Sweet Valley again."

Elizabeth gave Jessica a worried look.

"Be quiet, Zeek!" Gazeal commanded. "When I want your comments, I will ask for them. Until then, be silent."

Zeek moved back to his position against the wall.

"Don't worry," Gazeal told Andy and the Snoopers in a kind voice. "I'm sure you'll be able to solve the mystery. The Great Zard Council ordered me to bring home the best detectives in the universe. Everyone on my planet knows what great detectives earthlings are. If you can't help us, nobody can."

Elizabeth felt flattered, but she was also surprised. "Gazeal," Amy said carefully, "do you realize we are only children? Shouldn't you have kidnapped—I mean, *chosen* a chief of police? Or someone from Scotland Yard. You know, an *adult*."

"Children are just right to solve this mystery," Gazeal replied. "It involves the princess of our planet. Her name is Zari. The princess is just about the same age as all of you."

Zeek stepped forward and bowed to Gazeal.

She nodded to him. "You may speak."

"Zari's parents died many years ago," Zeek told Andy and the Snoopers. "Since that day our planet has been ruled by the wise and fair Gazeal, the princess's aunt. However, next week is Zari's eighth birthday. According to our laws it is time for the princess to take over the rule of Venn."

Gazeal picked up the tale. "Four earth-days ago a disaster occurred. Zari disappeared! You must find her. If you do not, an ancient decree says that the Nards get possession of Venn."

"The Nards?" Winston asked. "Who are they?"

"They are—" Zeek began.

"Evil creatures!" Gazeal interrupted. "The enemy of our people. The Nards love nothing but their weapons. Years ago they destroyed their own planet. They won't be happy until they have a new planet. No doubt the Nards kidnapped Zari. If you cannot find her in time, my people will lose their home."

"And you will never see Sweet Valley again," Zeek added.

CHAPTER 5

Exotic Landscape

Gazeal and Zeek left Andy and the Snoopers alone for the rest of the voyage. Nobody said much after they had gone. Each of the kids was busy thinking his or her own thoughts.

Jessica was hoping she would get to see her family and Sweet Valley again. But she did not have much time to feel homesick. Gazeal came to get Andy and the Snoopers after less than an hour. "We've arrived on Venn," Gazeal announced.

"I'm so excited," Andy told Jessica as they followed Gazeal and Zeek out of the ship. "We're about to see another planet. The scientists at NASA would be totally jealous!"

Jessica nodded. She didn't tell Andy how nervous she felt. What if Venn was covered with ice like that awful planet in the second *Star Wars* movie? What if there were man-eating beasts wandering around? What if there wasn't any air to breathe?

Elizabeth was walking in front of Jessica. "Oh," she sighed as she got her first view of Venn.

"It's beautiful," Jessica breathed.

The planet around them looked like a lush garden. Every inch of ground was covered with trees and flowering plants. But the plants weren't like the ones on earth—they were orange and purple.

"Look!" Amy said. "The ground is blue."

"I guess the sand you guys found didn't come from a fish tank," Winston said.

Amy grinned. "I guess not."

"We don't eat like humans do," Zeek warned the Snoopers. "We get all of the nutrients we need from the air. You won't need to eat while you are on Venn, and you should not try. The plants here could be poisonous for humans."

"Great," Jessica whispered to Elizabeth. "I'm starving. Air isn't going to make my stomach stop growling."

"Try not to think about it," Elizabeth suggested.

Gazeal led the way toward a white building topped with countless towers. "Our planet is much smaller than the earth," she told the earthlings. "You could walk around it in a day."

"But you have no time for sight-seeing," Zeek put in. "You have a mystery to solve."

"I wasn't suggesting they do anything other than look for the princess," Gazeal said. Her tone was sharp.

Zeek made a low bow. "Of course not, my lady."

Gazeal led Andy and the Snoopers past a guard, into the white building, and down a long hall. It was cool and quiet inside. Woven rugs covered the floor, and colorful paintings filled the walls.

"This is the ancient dwelling place of Venn's ruling family," Zeek told the earthlings.

"And these are your sleeping quarters," Gazeal added, opening the door. "Zeek, please make sure our guests are comfortable." She turned to Andy and the Snoopers. "I must go and make certain my people are safe. The Nards might have caused trouble while I was away. I'll talk to you later."

As soon as Gazeal was gone, an orange-haired Zard let himself into the room.

Zeek bowed very low and greeted him in Zardian.

"I am O'Hale, Zari's tutor," the new-comer told Andy and the Snoopers. "But what is this? You are mere children! What a joke! Gazeal was supposed to bring back the best detectives in the universe."

Before the Snoopers could answer, Zeek spoke up. "I didn't know you spoke English," he told O'Hale. "I thought only Gazeal and I—"

"You and Gazeal are not the only Zards who have ever visited earth," O'Hale replied. "I learned to speak English years ago. But please do not change the subject. Why has Gazeal brought these earthling children here?"

Zeek replied in Zardian.

Then O'Hale started to *yell* in Zardian.

Andy and the Snoopers had no idea what the aliens were saying. But they could not miss the angry tone.

"What's the deal with this O'Hale guy?" Todd whispered to the others.

"I don't think he's too happy to see us," Eva said.

"Why not?" Lila asked, shaking her head. "Gazeal said the Zards thought we were great detectives."

"I think he was expecting grown-ups," Ellen said.

"But Gazeal said—" Amy started.

"Listen," Winston interrupted. "I don't care if O'Hale is unhappy. Zeek said we're not going home until we find the princess. That means we better find her."

"The sooner the better," Elizabeth added.

Jessica nodded. Then she glanced at Zeek and O'Hale. They were still yelling at each other. Jessica agreed with Winston and Elizabeth, but the aliens weren't giving her much confidence.

CHAPTER 6

Inside the Royal Chamber

"Let's look for clues," Elizabeth said.

"All right," Ellen agreed. "Where should we start?"

"Wherever Zari was last seen," Eva suggested.

"I wonder where that was," Amy said.

The Snoopers turned to Zeek and O'Hale. They were still yelling.

Andy marched up to them. "If you don't mind, we'd like to start our investigation. Will one of you please show us the spot where Zari was last seen?"

Jessica smiled at Elizabeth. "Not bad."

"Andy would make a good Snooper," Elizabeth whispered.

"The princess was last seen in her sleeping chamber," O'Hale said.

"I'll show you the way," Zeek offered. He led them a few doors down the hall.

"Ooo," Jessica sighed as she followed Zeek and O'Hale into the princess's room.

A strange and beautiful creature was pacing the floor. It was the size of a large house cat, but had green and blue zebra stripes.

"What's that?" Lila asked.

"A belzam," O'Hale explained. "They are very intelligent and loyal creatures. Belzams live to protect their owners. Zari calls this one Ky. The two of them have been together many years."

"Gazeal told us Zari was kidnapped," Winston said.

"That's what *she* thinks," O'Hale said.

"Wouldn't Ky have protected her from

the kidnappers?" Winston asked.

O'Hale nodded. "If someone tried to kidnap the princess, Ky would have died trying to save her."

Winston frowned. "I don't understand."

Before O'Hale could reply, Todd called to Winston. "Come here!"

Winston hurried over to where Todd was standing.

"Look at this window," Todd told Winston. "There isn't a scratch on it. In fact, none of the room's windows and doors have been damaged."

Winston frowned. "But if the princess was kidnapped—"

"There would be signs of a struggle," Todd finished for him.

Elizabeth joined the boys. "Don't you think there's something interesting about Ky?"

"He's really cool," Todd said.

"Totally," Elizabeth agreed. "But that isn't the only thing. Look at the way he keeps rubbing up against that one part of the wall."

"So?" Winston asked.

"I don't know," Elizabeth said. "I just have a funny feeling it means something."

Elizabeth crept closer to the belzam and knelt down beside him. Ky jumped up and put his front paws on the wall. Elizabeth was positive the belzam was trying to tell her something. But what?

Ky jumped up and put his paws on the wall again. And again. Finally Elizabeth put her hands on the wall in the same spot. She pressed hard and gasped when a tiny drawer popped out.

Elizabeth peeked inside the drawer. She saw a small book with a clasp, like a diary. Elizabeth flipped the book open, but she couldn't read the writing. It looked like a series of dots.

Elizabeth brought the book to O'Hale,

who was watching Ellen and Jessica search under Zari's bed.

"Can you read this to me?" Elizabeth asked O'Hale. "Maybe it will give us a clue."

"Of course," O'Hale agreed, taking the book.

Andy, Zeek, and the Snoopers gathered around.

"Read the last thing she wrote," Jessica suggested.

O'Hale nodded and flipped a few pages. "I believe the greedy one will move before my birthday," he read. "I must find a safe place to hide. But where on Venn doesn't the greedy one have spies and allies? There is only one place. . . ."

"The greedy one?" Eva repeated. "Who could that be?"

"It sounds as if the princess was in trouble," Ellen said.

"She needed to hide," Jessica added.

"I don't think Zari was kidnapped,"

Winston said. "I think she ran away!"

Just then Elizabeth heard voices in the hallway.

"Gazeal is coming," Zeek whispered.

"I must leave you now," O'Hale told the earthlings. "Do not tell Gazeal we met."

"Why not?" Andy asked.

O'Hale did not answer. He slipped into a closet and closed the door. The Snoopers didn't have time to discuss his strange behavior. Gazeal swept in.

Elizabeth slipped the diary into her pocket.

"Have you made any progress?" Gazeal demanded.

The Snoopers exchanged looks.

Elizabeth stepped forward. "We didn't find anything important here. We'd like to search the planet for the princess."

"Of course," Gazeal said. "But you must understand a search will be dangerous. We must be careful. The Nards have spies everywhere. I will serve as your guide."

Gazeal led the Snoopers out of the room. Ky tried to follow them, but Gazeal shoved him inside and closed the door.

"Can't Ky come along?" Elizabeth asked. She had a feeling the belzam would be useful in their search.

"I'm afraid that's impossible," Gazeal said.

"Why?" Elizabeth asked.

"Do not forget that you are my guest on Venn," Gazeal replied. "I want the belzam to remain here. That's all the explanation you will get. It should be all the explanation you need."

"Sorry," Elizabeth said. She watched Gazeal walk to the head of the group and start to lead her friends down the hall.

"What's her problem?" Jessica whispered to Elizabeth.

"I don't know," Elizabeth said. "But I think we should keep an eye on her."

CHAPTER 7

Around and Around

"It's fascinating," Andy told Jessica.

"What?" Jessica asked.

The earthlings were following Gazeal down a street in the capital city. Gazeal stopped at each house or business and, in Zardian, questioned the aliens who lived or worked there. Gazeal told the earthlings nobody had seen the princess.

"In many ways the Zards have a more advanced civilization than we do," Andy said. "They can travel through space. And yet they don't have cars."

"It's better for us this way," Jessica

said. "It's hard to snoop from a car. Besides, Venn is a small planet."

"True," Andy said. "But you'd expect them to ride animals at least. Or do you think that's a development unique to earth?"

Jessica rolled her eyes. She had no idea what Andy was talking about. "Let's move closer to the front," she suggested. "I want to see what happens at this house."

"OK," Andy agreed.

Jessica and Andy crept forward as Gazeal knocked on the door of a small house.

A purple-haired Zard opened the door. She bowed many times to Gazeal. Then she did an extraordinary thing. She turned to Andy and the Snoopers and said, "Welcome, earthlings!"

"You speak English!" Elizabeth exclaimed.

The Zard smiled and nodded.

Jessica was psyched. So far they hadn't

been able to talk to any of the Zards they had met in their search.

"We are looking for the princess Zari," Lila said. "Have you—"

Gazeal interrupted in rapid and harsh-sounding Zardian.

The Zard seemed disturbed by Gazeal's words. She threw herself at Gazeal's feet.

"What's wrong?" Todd demanded.

The Zard looked up at the earthlings with sad eyes. She didn't say anything.

"She doesn't understand you," Gazeal said. "She only speaks a few words of English."

"What did you say to her?" Eva asked. "She seems upset."

"I did not upset her!" Gazeal exclaimed. "She is upset because of the Nards. She says they dipped her mother in hot oil."

"That's awful!" Ellen said.

"Why did the Nards do it?" Amy asked.

"She took a shortcut over Nard prop-

erty," Gazeal said. "The Nards consider trespassing a terrible crime."

"What a horrible story," Winston said.

The others murmured their agreement.

Gazeal translated many more horror stories for the Snoopers that afternoon. In the city a bald Zard said the Nards had plucked his hair out piece by piece because he had trespassed on their land.

A Zard child in the countryside said the Nards had caught her on their property and made her walk all the way home backward.

Nobody had seen Zari.

"Does this road look familiar?" Andy whispered to Jessica after they had been searching for hours.

"No," Jessica said. "Why?"

"Just a theory," Andy said. "I'm going to test it out." He took a lollipop out of his pocket.

"Food!" Jessica exclaimed. "Give it to me."

"Not yet," Andy said, pushing the lollipop stick into the blue sand. "You can have it later."

"What do you mean?" Jessica asked. "How can I have it if you're going to leave it behind?"

"Shh," Andy said. "I'm doing an experiment. Just wait and see."

Hours later Jessica spotted the lollipop in the distance. She pointed it out to Andy.

"Gazeal *is* leading us in circles," Andy said.

"No wonder we weren't finding anything," Jessica said.

"What do you think she's hiding?" Andy asked.

Jessica shook her head. "I don't know."

"What should we do?" Andy asked.

"Nothing yet," Jessica said.

Soon after that the sun started to go down.

"Our search of Venn is complete," Gazeal told the Snoopers. "Tomorrow you must begin to look for Zari off the planet. I will have Zeek take you in one of our ships."

"Did you show us all of Venn?" Andy asked.

"We have been everywhere," Gazeal insisted. "If there had been something to find, we would have found it."

Jessica and Andy exchanged looks. They knew the search had failed only because Gazeal had made sure of it.

Gazeal led Andy and the Snoopers back to their sleeping quarters. "I must go and prepare my people for war," she told the earthlings. "If Zari is not found by sundown tomorrow, the Nards will try to seize Venn. I will not surrender the planet without a fight."

"Don't worry," Andy told Gazeal. "We still have lots of searching to do."

51

"Please do your best to find Zari," Gazeal said to Andy and the Snoopers. "She is like a daughter to me. I couldn't go on without her."

CHAPTER 8

Lost

As soon as Gazeal was gone, Andy and Jessica told the others what they had discovered.

"I can't believe Gazeal lied to us," Ellen said.

"I don't think she wants Zari to be found," Elizabeth said.

"Then why would she bring the best detectives in the universe to Venn?" Todd asked.

Eva shook her head. "Remember how surprised O'Hale was when he saw us? He couldn't believe we were kids. Maybe

Gazeal brought us here because she thought we would *not* be able to find Zari."

"But why would she do that?" Amy asked. "Without Zari the Nards will take over Venn. And they sound mean."

"Gazeal said she was preparing the Zards for war," Lila pointed out. "Maybe she thinks she can beat the Nards."

"With Zari out of the way," Jessica said, "Gazeal could rule Venn herself."

"If that's her plan, she made a big mistake," Elizabeth said.

"Why?" Winston asked.

"Because we're going to find Zari," Elizabeth said.

"How?" Lila asked.

"We have to make a real search," Elizabeth said. "Tonight while Gazeal thinks we're asleep."

"How will we find our way around?" Todd asked.

"And how will we talk to the Zards?"

Winston added. "We don't speak their language."

"What if we run into the Nards?" Ellen asked.

Elizabeth shrugged. "Those are all good questions, and I don't have answers for them. But I still think we should try."

"I agree," Jessica said. "The princess is in trouble."

"Besides," Lila added, "if we don't solve the mystery, we don't go home."

Elizabeth bit her lip. She did not trust Gazeal to take them home even if they did solve the mystery. But she did not tell the others that.

The Snoopers waited until it was dark outside. Then they tiptoed out of their room.

Todd was in front because he thought he knew the way out of the palace. But in the darkness everything seemed changed. Andy and the Snoopers followed Todd from passageway to passageway without finding the way out.

Elizabeth was bringing up the rear of the group. She felt hopeless. She was exhausted from walking all day. She missed home, and she was worried she would never see it again.

Just as Elizabeth was about to suggest they give up, someone grabbed her from behind. She tried to scream, but her mouth was covered by a strong hand.

"Keep quiet!" Elizabeth's attacker whispered. "It's me, Zeek. I'm going to help you find your way out of the palace. But you must not say a word."

Slowly, Zeek released Elizabeth.

Elizabeth wasn't sure what to do. She did not trust Zeek. But the Snoopers needed help. Silently, Elizabeth tapped each of the Snoopers on the shoulder. She motioned for them to follow her and Zeek. Elizabeth could only hope she was not leading her friends into danger.

CHAPTER 9

Danger

Zeek ushered Andy and the Snoopers into Zari's room. "You are in danger," he whispered. "Someone wants you out of the way. If you don't get out of the palace now, you will never leave."

"Who wants us out of the way?" Jessica asked.

"Someone powerful," Zeek said.

"Is it Gazeal?" Elizabeth asked.

Zeek didn't say anything for a minute. Then he nodded. "Gazeal wants Venn for her own. She wouldn't mind killing you to get it. You have to get out of here. Hurry!"

As the Snoopers were hurrying out, Jessica felt Ky jump onto her shoulder. She found his presence reassuring.

Zeek led the earthlings out of the palace. In the square outside, hundreds of Zards had gathered. They were carrying weapons and wearing dark capes.

"Gazeal is preparing us for war," Zeek whispered to the earthlings. "It will be the first war on Venn in more than two thousand years."

Zeek led the earthlings down the dark streets of the capital city. He stopped in front of a brightly lit building.

"Wait here for a Zard named Saleel," Zeek told them. "He does not speak much English, but he is a friend. He will take you to safety."

Before the earthlings could ask any questions, Zeek hurried off.

Andy and the Snoopers hid themselves as well as possible in the shadows near the building. It sounded as if hundreds of Zards were inside and they were all yelling at once. The noise was loud and frightening. Jessica decided it must be some kind of alien bar.

Zards came and went, but none approached the Snoopers. The sky was beginning to lighten when a huge Zard came out of the bar. Ky jumped off Jessica's shoulder and rubbed against his legs. Wordlessly, the Zard motioned for Andy and the Snoopers to follow him.

The earthlings fell into line behind him.

I hope this is Saleel, Jessica thought.

Andy and the Snoopers followed the Zard for a long time. The sun was starting to rise, and they had reached a city they had not seen on their search the day before.

This city was not as beautiful as the capital. A tall, dark stone wall surrounded it. Outside the wall empty blue sand stretched in all directions.

"Where are we?" Jessica wondered out loud.

Saleel pointed to the city. "Nard city. Go in."

The earthlings exchanged terrified looks.

"Nard city," Saleel repeated. "Go in."

"The princess can't be in there," Lila said.

"The Nards are dangerous," Eva said.

Saleel didn't seem to be listening. He turned and started back across the sand.

Andy and the Snoopers stared at each other. They weren't sure what to do.

"This could be a trap," Andy pointed out. "Maybe Zeek wanted to get rid of us."

"Maybe Zeek is working for Gazeal," Winston suggested.

Todd nodded. "He is always all bows and smiles when she is around."

"I have a bad feeling about this," Amy said.

"What are we going to do?" Ellen asked. Tears were welling up in her eyes.

"We're stuck in the middle of nowhere on a strange planet. We can't trust anybody. We're probably never going to get home."

Before anyone could answer Ellen, Ky jumped off Jessica's shoulder. He darted through the gate and into the city.

"Ky, come back!" Jessica cried. She ran after him.

Jessica's heart was pounding as she passed through the gate. She was well aware she was trespassing in the city of the Nards.

CHAPTER 10

Inside the Nard Colony

Elizabeth watched Jessica disappear into the Nard city. "I'm going after her," she yelled, starting to run.

"Wait!" Todd shouted. "It's too dangerous."

Elizabeth didn't stop. She ran through the gate. Elizabeth could see Jessica standing in the middle of a stone street with buildings lining the sides. She was holding Ky.

Elizabeth ran to Jessica's side. "Are you all right?"

"I'm fine," Jessica said.

Andy and the rest of the Snoopers ran up to the twins.

"We decided we better not split up," Amy explained.

Andy and the Snoopers glanced around the street. A couple of aliens spotted the earthlings and hurried off.

"Do you see any Nards?" Ellen asked.

"No," Todd said. "All I see are Zards. But there is something strange about them."

"Who cares?" Lila said. "Let's get out of here before the Nards come."

"Good idea," Winston agreed.

The Snoopers hurried back down the street. But before they reached the gate, a group of aliens approached them.

"Run!" Eva yelled.

It was too late. One of the aliens grabbed Ellen's arms.

Ellen kicked her feet with all her might. "Get off me! Let go!"

Lila tried to pry the alien's fingers off

Ellen's arm. Jessica stomped on the alien's foot. But it was no use. He wouldn't let go.

Other aliens grabbed Lila, Jessica, and the rest of the earthlings. They dragged them back up the street.

"Where are you taking us?" Elizabeth demanded.

The aliens grunted something in what sounded like Zardian.

"They probably don't speak English," Andy said.

"Do you think they're taking us to the Nards?" Eva asked, struggling against the alien who was holding her.

Nobody answered that one.

The aliens took Andy and the Snoopers into a building and left them in a big room. The floor was covered with soft material and pillows. The Snoopers were exhausted, but they were afraid to sleep. They were dreading their first sight of a Nard. After what seemed like a long time, the door opened and a single alien entered. Its face was hidden behind a hood. As soon as the alien entered the room, Ky went wild.

"Don't be afraid," Jessica whispered to the belzam, struggling to control him.

"What are you earthlings doing here?" the alien demanded.

"We seek the princess Zari," Elizabeth answered.

"Gazeal's spies are not welcome here," the alien said.

"We aren't spies," Todd said. "Gazeal brought us to Venn to find the princess. But she doesn't know we are here in the city of the Nards."

Just then Jessica lost her battle with the belzam. He jumped out of her arms and ran toward the alien.

"Ky, no!" Jessica yelled.

The belzam paid no attention to Jessica. He rubbed up against the alien's legs and then jumped onto the alien's shoulder.

The alien made a noise that sounded like a laugh. "Ky, cut it out. You're giving me away." With that the alien removed the hood.

Elizabeth expected to see a hideous Nard. But this creature was beautiful. She had huge green eyes. Her shiny purple hair was piled on top of her head. She was wearing a necklace that shone like a diamond.

Elizabeth watched Ky with the beautiful alien. The belzam was acting like a puppy whose master has just come home. Elizabeth guessed they had found their princess. "You must be Zari," she said.

"Yes, I am," Zari said. "How did you find me?"

"We had help from Zeek," Andy said.

"And O'Hale," Todd said.

"And Ky," Jessica added.

Zari frowned. "I see you know all of my friends."

"We also know you came here on your own," Elizabeth said. She pulled Zari's diary

out of her pocket and handed it to the princess. "O'Hale translated part of this for us."

"You went to a lot of trouble to find me," Zari said. "I hope you understand I cannot go back to the capital."

"But you must," Elizabeth insisted. "You're in danger here. The Nards might arrive any moment."

"What do you mean?" Zari asked. "The Nards brought you here."

"B-but—" Eva stammered.

"You must be mistaken," Amy spoke up. "The guards who brought us here looked just like Zards."

"Of course they did," Zari said. "The only difference between Zards and Nards is that Zards have green eyes and Nards have yellow ones."

"Aren't you afraid of them?" Lila asked.

"No," Zari said. She seemed puzzled by the Snoopers' questions. "The Nards are a peaceful people. They do not even have an army or weapons."

"Gazeal told us they dipped trespassers in hot oil," Ellen said. "And plucked out their hairs one at a time."

Zari frowned. "Then Gazeal lied."

"She told us the Nards blew up their planet," Andy said.

"That is not true," Zari said. "The Nards used to live on Venn's sister planet, Nev. Venn and Nev revolve around the same sun and share two moons.

"Many years ago a huge asteroid hit Nev. Overnight the planet grew cold. Ice covered everything. My mother, who ruled Venn at that time, invited the surviving Nards to live with us on Venn. The Zards and Nards lived together in peace until Gazeal forced the Nards to move to this remote city."

"Nev didn't blow up?" Andy asked.

"No," Zari said. "We have a small outpost there. Scientists are working to repair the environment, but it is still cold and dark."

The Snoopers exchanged glances.

"Zari," Winston said, "your people are preparing for war against the Nards."

Zari's beautiful eyes widened. "I don't understand."

"Gazeal has told the Zards that the Nards are trying to take control of Venn," Jessica explained.

"If you don't go back," Ellen said, "the Nards will be wiped out."

"You are the only one who can stop the war," Eva said.

"You're right," Zari said without hesitation. "I must go home right away."

"We're coming, too," Amy said.

"Coming with me could be dangerous," Zari said. "There's no telling what Gazeal might do. I think you should discuss it among yourselves first."

The Snoopers discussed it. Everyone agreed. They had to return to the capital city and help Zari defeat Gazeal.

CHAPTER 11

The Brink of War

"How are you doing?" Elizabeth asked Jessica.

"Fine," Jessica said. "But I feel like Darth Vader in this cape."

Elizabeth smiled. "You might look like him, but you don't *sound* like him."

"That's a relief," Jessica said.

Zari, Andy, and the Snoopers were walking toward the capital city. Zari had insisted the earthlings dress in long, dark capes with hoods. She said they needed a good disguise.

Six Nards were with them, too. Zari had

tried to convince the Nards to stay behind. The princess said they were putting themselves in great danger by entering the capital city. But the Nards refused to allow Zari and the earthlings to go alone.

The group reached the capital at sundown. They hurried through the streets toward the palace. The city was full of Zards readying themselves for battle. Hiding behind her hood, Jessica stared at the Zards' weapons. They sent chills up her spine. She knew Zari and the Nards were unarmed.

Zari led the group into the palace through a secret entrance. The first Zard they met was O'Hale.

Zari removed her hood and greeted him.

O'Hale gave Zari a hug. "Where have you been, my dear? I've been frantic with worry."

"Hiding," Zari told him. "But the earthlings found me and brought me home. It's

74

a good thing you made me learn English."

"The earthlings?" O'Hale sounded amazed, but he did not ask any questions. He took the princess's hands in his. "Zari, you arrived just in time. We are on the brink of war. You must stop Gazeal. Follow me."

O'Hale hurried down the hall. Zari, the Nards, Andy, and the Snoopers rushed after him. O'Hale led Zari, Andy, and the Snoopers to a large room. Gazeal, Zeek, and many fierce-looking Zards were inside.

As soon as Zeek saw the princess, he threw himself at her feet. "Praise to the earthlings! They have found you."

"Hi, Zeek," Zari said with a smile.

Gazeal seemed shocked. "Welcome, Zari," she finally managed to say. "I'm glad to see you are safe. Unfortunately, it is too late for you to take over the rule of Venn. We are on the brink of war."

"No, we're not," Zari said.

"I do not have time for this foolishness,"

Gazeal said, motioning to the guards. "Take the princess to her room. She's getting in the way. I have a battle to plan."

The guards approached Zari. But before they could touch her, the Nards stepped forward. They stood between the guards and the princess. Zeek joined the Nards.

Gazeal strode up to the first Nard and pulled off his hood. "Look!" Gazeal exclaimed. "Zari is a traitor. She has led the enemy into our midst. Kill the Nards and the earthlings. Take the princess away."

The guards drew their weapons.

"Wait!" Zari yelled. "The Nards are not our enemies. They came here unarmed. They only want peace."

The guards searched the Nards. They found no weapons. The guards took a step back and began to whisper among themselves.

"There is no need for a battle," Zari said.

"This girl wants the Nards to overrun us!" Gazeal screeched. "I tell you she is a traitor!"

"You are the traitor," Zari told Gazeal. "You are spreading hatred among our people. I think you could use some time alone to think about what you've done. That is why I am sending you to Nev. Five years in the ice should help you cool off. Now go to your room and pack some warm clothes."

One of the guards led Gazeal out.

"Inform the soldiers the attack has been canceled," Zari told Zeek. "And give them the rest of the week off."

The next day Zari was crowned queen of Venn.

Everyone on the entire planet—Zards and Nards alike—was invited to a party in honor of the new queen.

Andy and the Snoopers had a terrific time. They listened to Zard music and danced with the Nards. Zeek told the earthlings stories about his travels in the universe. O'Hale taught them how to count to five in Zardian.

When the party was over, Zari invited the earthlings to remain on Venn as her guests.

"It's a wonderful offer," Jessica told the queen. "And I know I'm going to miss my new friends, but I want to go home."

Elizabeth, Andy, and the rest of the Snoopers agreed.

Zari smiled sadly. "If that is your wish, I will take you there myself."

The earthlings said good-bye to O'Hale, Ky, and Zeek.

"I owe you all an apology," O'Hale told the Snoopers. "I thought you could not be good detectives just because you were children. You have proved how wrong I was."

"Does this mean we really are the best

detectives in the universe?" Todd asked Elizabeth.

Elizabeth smiled. "You had doubts?"

"I also underestimated you," Zeek told the earthlings. "I threatened you because I thought you would do a better job finding the princess if you were afraid you would never see your home again."

Eva laughed. "You definitely had us worried."

Jessica took one last look at Venn. And then, smiling through her tears, she followed Zari onboard the ship.

CHAPTER 12

There's No Place Like Home

"I can see the earth!" Elizabeth exclaimed.

"That's North America," Andy said, pointing.

Zari and the earthlings gathered around the spaceship's window. They were speeding toward the earth.

"There's New York!" Todd said. "I see the Statue of Liberty!"

"Hey, Zari," Andy said. "We need to go farther west."

"Oops," Zari said. "Sorry."

Seconds later the ship zipped over the Grand Canyon.

"That's Los Angeles," Amy cried.

"How did you turn the ship?" Todd asked Zari. "I didn't see you push a button or anything."

"There aren't any buttons," Zari told him. "I just have to think a command, and the ship follows it."

"Neat," Winston said. The others nodded in agreement.

"There's Sweet Valley," Ellen said.

"That patch of blue must be Secca Lake," Eva said.

Jessica grinned. "We're almost home."

"Do you think our parents are still waiting for us?" Elizabeth asked quietly.

"We have been gone an awfully long time," Amy said.

"What if years and years have gone by?" Lila whispered. "Maybe our families have forgotten all about us."

Suddenly Andy and the Snoopers got very quiet.

"Don't worry," Zari told the earthlings. "Everything will be fine."

Elizabeth wanted to ask Zari how she knew. Instead she yawned an enormous yawn. Suddenly Elizabeth felt very sleepy.

Zari gave Andy and each of the Snoopers a hug good-bye. She thanked them again for their help.

Elizabeth had a thousand questions she wanted to ask Zari, but she was too tired to talk. Elizabeth closed her eyes. They had already been gone a long, long time. It wouldn't matter much if she took a short nap. . . .

Elizabeth opened her eyes and waved a bug away from her face. The sun was shining down through green leaves on the trees. Birds were chirping. Elizabeth sat up. She had just had the most extraordinary dream. Elizabeth could remember it all—Venn, the beautiful alien princess, evil Gazeal, and Ky.

Jessica sat up and rubbed her eyes. Andy, Amy, and the rest of the Snoopers were waking up, too.

"I just had the most wonderful dream," Jessica announced. "You were all in it."

"I had a dream, too," Elizabeth said. "We were kidnapped by aliens."

"That's what happened in *my* dream," Jessica said. "We dreamed the same thing."

"I don't think so," Elizabeth said. "I think it happened."

Andy and the Snoopers were all listening to the twins.

"Tell us about your dream," Amy suggested.

"There was a princess, and she . . . ," Elizabeth started. But as she started to tell the others about their adventure, she realized her memory of it had gotten fuzzy. She frowned, trying to remember.

"She had an evil aunt," Jessica said. "And—and the ground was blue!"

Todd laughed. "You dreamed about blue sand because we found that pile of it."

"Maybe," Jessica said.

Andy spoke up. "I remember it, too," he said. "The aliens were green."

"See?" Jessica said. "It did happen!"

"That doesn't prove anything," Winston said. "Andy thought he saw a green alien two days ago. He put the idea in your minds."

"Maybe," Andy admitted. "But don't you feel kind of funny?"

Eva nodded. "I feel like I just woke up from taking a nap in the middle of the day. I haven't taken a nap in years."

"That's another thing," Elizabeth said. "Don't you think it's strange that we all fell asleep?"

Amy shrugged. "We probably got too much sun. That always makes me sleepy."

Lila stood up. "Who cares? Let's eat."

"Good idea," Jessica agreed as she got to her feet. "I'm starved."

"I could eat a pound of potato salad," Amy said.

"Wait!" Jessica called out. She leaned over and scooped something up off the ground. "Look what I found!"

The others gathered around.

"That's Zari's necklace," Elizabeth said. "She must have left it for us."

"Who's Zari?" Ellen asked.

"The alien princess," Elizabeth said.

Lila rolled her eyes. "Jessica probably saw the necklace before she fell asleep. That's why it became part of her dream."

"But—" Andy started.

"Last one down is a rotten egg!" Winston shouted.

Everyone started to run. When the Snoopers got to the bottom of the trail, they found Mrs. Wakefield, Mrs. Franklin, and Mr. Sutton laying out the food. The

kids flopped down on the picnic blanket.

"Why isn't anyone sitting next to Andy?" Mr. Sutton asked.

Jessica pinched her nose. "Rotten eggs stink!"

Everyone laughed. Even Andy.

"Did you see any aliens?" Mrs. Wakefield asked as she passed the plates.

"Of course not!" Todd said.

Elizabeth and Jessica exchanged looks.

"I thought that's why you guys dragged us out to the lake," Mr. Sutton said.

"Don't be weird, Dad," Amy said. "Everyone knows there's no such thing as creatures from outer space."

Elizabeth was about to disagree, but before she could get a word out, Jessica poked her.

"Would you please pass me a sandwich?" Jessica asked.

"You already have one," Elizabeth pointed out.

"I know," Jessica said. "But I'm really hungry. I feel as if I haven't eaten in days."

"Maybe you haven't," Elizabeth said.

Jessica reached up and touched the necklace around her neck. "Maybe not."

SIGN UP FOR THE SWEET VALLEY HIGH® FAN CLUB!

Hey, girls! Get all the gossip on Sweet Valley High's® most popular teenagers when you join our fantastic Fan Club! As a member, you'll get all of this really cool stuff:

- Membership Card with your own personal Fan Club ID number
- A Sweet Valley High® Secret Treasure Box
- Sweet Valley High® Stationery
- Official Fan Club Pencil (for secret note writing!)
- Three Bookmarks
- A "Members Only" Door Hanger
- Two Skeins of J. & P. Coats® Embroidery Floss with flower barrette instruction leaflet
- Two editions of *The Oracle* newsletter
- Plus exclusive Sweet Valley High® product offers, special savings, contests, and much more!

Be the first to find out what Jessica & Elizabeth Wakefield are up to by joining the Sweet Valley High® Fan Club for the one-year membership fee of only $6.25 each for U.S. residents, $8.25 for Canadian residents (U.S. currency). Includes shipping & handling.

Send a check or money order (do not send cash) made payable to "Sweet Valley High® Fan Club" along with this form to:

SWEET VALLEY HIGH® FAN CLUB, BOX 3919-B, SCHAUMBURG, IL 60168-3919

NAME_____
(Please print clearly)

ADDRESS_____

CITY_____ STATE_____ ZIP_____
(Required)

AGE_____ BIRTHDAY_____ /_____ /_____

Offer good while supplies last. Allow 6-8 weeks after check clearance for delivery. Addresses without ZIP codes cannot be honored. Offer good in USA & Canada only. Void where prohibited by law.
©1993 by Francine Pascal   LCI-1383-123